Why the Sun &

Moon

live in the Sky

For Jude ~ my other half,
with love ~ Niki.

The illustrations in this book were done in watercolor paints.
The display type was hand-lettered by Andrew van der Merwe.
The text was set in Bernhard Modern. Printed and bound by South China.
Production supervision by Linda Palladino. Designed by Niki Daly.

First Edition   1 2 3 4 5 6 7 8 9 10

Library of Congress Cataloging in Publication Data
Daly, Niki. Why the Sun and Moon live in the sky / by Niki Daly.
p.   cm. Summary: Sun and Moon must leave their earthly home after Sun invites the Sea to visit.
ISBN 0-688-13331-2. — ISBN 0-688-13332-0 (lib. bdg.)   [1. Folklore—Nigeria. 2. Sun—Folklore. 3. Moon—Folklore.]
I. Title. PZ8.1.D17Wh 1994 398.2—dc20 [E] 93-47304 CIP AC

Niki Daly

✩

Why the
Sun & Moon
live in the Sky

Lothrop, Lee & Shepard Books   New York

There was once a time when Sun and Moon lived on the earth.

Their grand house stood on a mountaintop overlooking endless grasslands, fiery deserts, distant mountains, and fiercely chiseled valleys. Just on the silver rim, where the earth curved away from sight, lived Sea.

Sun, a traveler and seeker of beauty, loved to roam over the skin
of the earth.

Moon, content to enjoy the things placed before her by the
Great Creator, remained at home.

Sun had seen many of the earth's great wonders, but none
pleased him more than Sea. Her spellbinding songs and her
liquid dances compelled him to visit her often.

"Sea, you are so very beautiful," sighed Sun. "I would like Moon to see your splendor. We have a very fine house, and you would be a welcome guest."

"It would have to be very large as well as fine," murmured Sea. "For where I go, go all my children."

"My house is as broad as it is wide, and higher than that!" boasted Sun.

"Seeing is believing," whispered Sea.

"Then do come and see for yourself," urged Sun eagerly. So it was decided that Sea and all her children would visit the great home of Sun and Moon.

When Sun returned home, he told Moon all about the beautiful Sea, soon to be their guest. "You will see how magnificent she is," exclaimed the infatuated Sun. "She shimmers and dances without end. And her songs are as soothing as sleep."

"Does she plan to bring *all* her children?" inquired Moon.

"The greatest and the smallest," answered Sun.

Moon gazed at all her pretty things and turned blue at the
thought of such a visit.

Sooner than expected, Sea arrived, carrying all her slippery, scaled, and shelled children in her writhing belly. They came roaring and thrashing, whooshing and crashing, right up to the front door. "Come in, come in!" cried the welcoming Sun.

In Sea flowed, bringing with her a collection of starfish, sea
urchins, and mussels. Her skirts lapped against the walls. "May
I bring in my finned children?" she asked.

"Yes, yes," sang the rapturous Sun, ankle-deep in frothy water.

Moon stood stonily and grumbled, "What kind of guest is
this who spreads herself all over my house?"

Sea flowed wildly through the vast corridors and chambers.
Great squids and whales from her lower depths swirled up to the
surface to admire the house of Sun and Moon.

"Will your house really hold *all* my children?" asked Sea.

Sun was no longer certain, but he did not wish to appear mean. "Never let it be said that Sun turned away *any* of Sea's children," he pronounced. "Come in, come in!"

Sea churned and foamed as she lashed about, filling the entire house. Her children explored in and out of chambers and cupboards, making themselves at home. Now Sea was in the house and the house was in her, but still she kept arriving.

"Sun," scolded Moon, "you have done something very foolish by inviting Sea into our home! Look! She is as wide as she is deep, and she is most unpredictable."

Higher and higher swelled Sea. Higher and higher climbed Sun and Moon . . . until they reached the sky. And that's where they have remained ever since—looking down over the beautiful and bounteous Sea.

But the disenchanted Moon could no longer bear to live with
the fool Sun. So instead she lives with her star children on the
dark side of time, where Sun and Moon never meet.

This is my story, which I have related, if it be sweet, or if it be not sweet~take some elsewhere and let some come back to me. ~N.D.